Make No Mistakes

Sophisticated Devices

# JESSE MICHAELS
## Make No Mistakes

# SAM McPHEETERS
## Sophisticated Devices

BARNACLE SPLIT EDITIONS

RARE BIRD BOOKS
LOS ANGELES, CALIF.

*Sam McPheeters thanks Paul Maliszewski and Jesse Pearson for their help.*

THIS IS A GENUINE BARNACLE BOOK

A Barnacle Book | Rare Bird Books
453 South Spring Street, Suite 302
Los Angeles, CA 90013
rarebirdbooks.com

Set in Minion
Printed in the United States

10 9 8 7 6 5 4 3 2 1

Publisher's Cataloging-in-Publication data

Michaels, Jesse, 1969-
Sophisticated devices : make no mistake / by Jesse Michaels and Sam McPheeters.
pages cm
ISBN 978-1-942600-04-6

1. Child molesters—Fiction. 2. Sex offenders—Fiction. 3. Probation—Fiction. 4. Shopping malls—Fiction. 5. Cults—Fiction. 6. Psychotherapy—Fiction. I. McPheeters, Sam. II. Title.

PS3613.I34436 S67 2015
813.6 —dc23

## *Barnacle Split Editions*

*Barnacle and Rare Bird are proud to introduce to you the first in a very special series of books that adapts the idea of split release records to books. Ladies and gentlemen, Barnacle Split Editions...*

Sophisticated Devices

by Sam McPheeters

# At

noon, two guards evicted Chang from his cell. He followed them across the gentle curve of the U ward mezzanine, down the south stairs to a smoothed rainbow mural, a leftover from the days when the wing had been a day-care annex for prison employees. A guard entered magic codes into a keypad, one final event of regulation life. As the rainbow folded inward on its own huge hinges, Chang realized some of the mural had faded during his own time in prison, and he finally saw this eviction for what it really was: an escape. He had outlasted his opponent, carefully minding his days and years until someone in an office somewhere had said uncle. It was a victory of attrition.

The rainbow opened onto a corridor, and the corridor opened onto a fenced-off patch of parking lot, an outdoor walkway connecting building units. "Pick one," a guard said without conviction, nudging a chin at two dirty plastic lawn chairs. Chang perched on the cigarette-scarred seat holding less rainwater. He signed a line on the clipboard and the guards were gone, closing the door behind them with several inorganic clunks, as if they didn't trust him not to creep back in. This was the holding pen of legal limbo. He looked out across the expanse of parking lot before him, taking in the heat shimmering from parked cars, the fence in the foreground. He hadn't seen as quaint a barrier as chain-link since the blazing, cicada-filled morning in 2010 when he'd first entered the penal system. The slightest of breezes now reached him, and he pictured himself on that afternoon, having been led through fences, drawn toward the core of horror, wild-eyed with possibilities.

Attrition. He'd written letters to everyone in his family that terrible first week, trying to explain. *If anyone has ever thought up any good ways to escape from prison*, he'd closed each letter, only half joking, *now would be the time to test those ideas out.* Three weeks later he'd received a postcard from his aunt Katie, a neatly scripted one-liner—*Attrition*—that had served as the first and last word from anyone he'd ever known. Behind several feet of concrete, a muted lunch bell now rang. He'd been a free man for fifteen minutes.

At a quarter to one, Warden Ball appeared from the connecting building and waved him in. In the dimmed fluorescents of the office, Chang saw only the outlines of filing cabinets, stacks of boxes in the corners, Ball's girth settling behind a desk.

"Please," said the warden, motioning to another plastic chair. The man absently poked through loose piles of documents on his desk. Chang had dreamed about this room, but never like this, subject to the same laws of cinderblock crumminess as the rest of his world. No plaques, no stag heads, no wall of shanks. Ball squinted into a piece of paper and announced, "Sheldon S. Chanfeld, having completed his eighteen-year prison term in full and to the satisfaction of the state of New Jersey…"

As Chang's eyes adjusted, a bulletin board on the far wall emerged with a slow fade-in, revealing a beautiful montage of Ball's vacation pictures. He sat very still, taking it all in. A room he'd never been in before. Blue skies, mountain streams, smiling men in hip waders and canvas hats enjoying life for what it is, free to move beyond the edges of the photographs.

The enormity of what was transpiring settled in on him, the horizons of his own life suddenly revealed, all things possible.

"Sheldon, did you hear me?"

"Yes," said Chang. "No. Sorry."

"I said, 'This state has a Jimmy Law.'"

"Okay."

"And you do understand what this means?"

"No."

Ball shared a stagy glance with the filing cabinets.

"Sheldon. Haven't you seen the news or read a paper in the last ten years?"

"No," said Chang. "We're not allowed TV or papers in the U."

Ball stared for a moment, his mouth an oval. "Of course," he finally laughed, bouncing a palm off his forehead. "That's part of the Jimmy Law!"

A mass rose in Chang's peripheral vision. "Sheldon, this is Mr. Morton, your parole officer."

He turned, startled, to see a huge, suited black man standing in a space he'd thought filled with clutter. Morton's head was crisply shaved, and his parallel accessories—thin spectacles, thin mustache, rigid purple bow tie—spoke to an order of authority Chang was exceedingly familiar with.

"Good morning, Mr. Chanfield. I'm here to explain the rules. You do want to understand the rules, don't you?"

Chang shook the man's hand, nodding slowly, still pivoted in his chair. Morton continued: "As you are now aware, the voters of this state have passed a Jimmy Law. This law places six stipulations on your release." Morton folded his hands carefully in front of him. "You will be living in a halfway house for the first eighteen months of your parole period. You will not be allowed any contact with minors, be it verbal, physical, or electronic." Morton unfurled a meaty finger for each provision. "You will register with the state police as a sex offender." Ball handed him a sheaf of forms, blue and yellow and pink.

"You will remain on mandatory prescription to a chemical hormone blocker of the court's discretion, to be administered by automatic injection."

Chang bobbed his head.

"Jimmy's Law also stipulates that your immediate community be notified at all times of your presence," Morton said, reaching into a canvas bag next to the couch. "And so…" He pulled something made of cloth from the bag, a strange bundle that reminded Chang of a Christmas tree skirt. Warden Ball perched himself on a corner of the desk. Morton unfurled the cloth. Chang understood that this was a T-shirt, but the material itself was alive with a garish TV glow, the garment casting its own light. On the front of the shirt, large, blinking red letters spelled out I AM A CONVICTED SEX OFFENDER. From behind, Warden Ball said, "That is so neat."

Morton looked at Chang without expression and then down to the illuminated T-shirt. After ten or fifteen seconds, the shirt went momentarily blank, then flashed a new message: PLEASE GUARD YOUR CHILDREN. "See," Morton explained, fumbling with the cloth, "the front of the shirt is imbedded with thousands of light pixels. There's a small battery in there… somewhere…"

Chang looked to the warden, then back to his new probation officer. Morton placed the blinking shirt on the couch and abruptly dropped to one knee like a shoe store clerk, gingerly producing a black rubber anklet fastened to a small box. He placed a dozen or so ampoules of sinister green into this tiny chamber, sealing it with a half-twist of his oversized thumb.

"You were taking Depo-Lupron?" Morton asked, fully turning Chang and securing the device around a pale ankle.

"Um…yeah."

"This stuff is stronger," the man said, looking up, still grasping the silly, skinny limb.

"The law also makes your employment mandatory. Let me ask you something, Mister Chanfield. Do you have any prospects for employment?"

Chang shook his head.

"Do you have any relatives or friends who might be able to provide you with gainful employment?"

Chang looked at the shirt. "*No.*"

"Well then," Morton continued, standing slowly, repositioning his center of gravity. "We will have to get you a job."

The two-story halfway house sat on the edge of a dead lot in an unincorporated tract of land north of Linden. Chang wondered if they had given this place a name yet, or if it had ever had one before. The outside of the house stank of skunk. Morton and two state troopers chaperoned him into the front kitchen, the foam panels of the drop ceiling popping out of place as the door slammed behind them, little eddies of cat fur swirling momentarily in the corner. On a shelf thick with orange paint, Chang noticed a familiar array of prison commissary staples: hard candies, ramen, Spam, Tang.

A squat old lady signed a form on another clipboard, a bill of lading, and Morton was off. "I *will* call you in the morning, Sheldon," he said, pulling the door shut behind him. Chang stood at attention, holding his small box of toiletries and folded clothes. He expected an introduction or instructions, but the old woman only muttered, walking down the hall. He followed her past a doorless lavatory, to a room next to the stairs. "Yeah, see," she offered, "they always release you guys on Sundays. And that really screws us up." They stood like this for a moment, at the threshold of his new room, and then she continued up the stairs, leaving him behind. In the room he found a bed, an open closet, a chipboard dresser that once had handles. He understood there were no doors here, no way to hide wrongdoing. The loose metal frame of the box spring swayed beneath his weight. He missed the stainless steel furnishings of cell U-42—the safe little submarine berth he would never see again.

Later that afternoon, a deliveryman made him sign yet another form on yet another clipboard. This was for a week and a half's supply of electronic T-shirts, each sheathed in warm dry cleaners' plastic. Chang carefully hung the shirts in his narrow closet and laid on the bed for a long while, watching the words blink out of time with each other, the plastic and coat hangers and flaking closet walls lit in endless combinations of pink and shadow. At some point he must have dozed off. Later, Chang saw another man in the doorway also watching the small light display in his closet, the stranger's own shirt announcing his guilt to the waking world in great, blinking Helvetica: CAUTION—I AM A POTENTIAL SEXUAL PREDATOR.

THERE HAD BEEN AN attack a week before his sentencing. He'd overheard his public defender discussing the matter with a bailiff in amused whispers. He still remembered the man's name—Freddie Bolson. On the second night of a twelve-year term for child pornography, someone in general population had torn out Freddie's throat with a jagged wedge of aluminum. There were no witnesses.

That had been the first night Chang had really cried—not the showy sobs of his arrest, but a private, keening wail he'd not known himself capable of, a death song from his throat, his eyes, all the tender spots of his body. But after the sentencing, his attorney had explained that there had been a trajectory change. Bolson's sacrifice meant Chang's survival. He would be held in a new wing for protective custody. He had been rerouted.

THE NEXT MORNING, MORTON called on the hall phone and gave instructions for the city bus. Chang made some instant coffee and carefully slid into the shirt, finding it heavy and strangely cold, as if wet. Next to the kitchen he found a wood-paneled room holding bare, discolored cloth couches. No one was home. When there was nothing else to do and no more time to linger, he stood by the front door for a long moment, remembering Freddie Bolson, tenderly caressing the knob as if he could coax the house into allowing him to stay.

Nothing happened on the two-block walk. The bus stop, deserted, hid no ambush. The driver looked at the awful words on his shirt and pointed to a small slot for dollar bills. Fellow riders bobbed along indifferently. Public transportation brought Chang through neighborhoods that looked distinctly familiar, and at a particular intersection he stepped out into welcoming sunlight. Boxy cars raced past toward more pressing matters. Across an expanse of asphalt he saw his destination, a shopping mall he distantly remembered attending in a past life.

Morton waited inside. He made a motion for Chang to follow, leading him through a wide corridor of unlit vending machines to an empty concourse. "You are now an employee of Pretzel Connection, Sheldon." Morton pointed to a small food stand, bracketed by comically oversized wagon wheels and shielded by a large cloth umbrella from the overhead air duct. Chang circled the food cart, finding a fresh paper hat and still another clipboard thick with forms. "These," Morton said, resting one finger on the paperwork, "you will need to read." Chang nodded.

"Money goes in this lockbox here, Sheldon. You do not accept tipping. Bus schedules, wages, your W-2, lunch times, supervisor phone numbers? It is all included on your clipboard. There's a map of the mall that way," Morton pointed, not smiling. "You will not enter the mall any lower than level six. That injection anklet you wear has a tracking device on it. I can tell where your leg is anywhere in this state, give or take a foot. I can be here in three and a half minutes. That's clocked. I find your leg below level six? I find you loitering where you're not supposed to? I will kill you. Believe that I have that authority. Do you understand?"

Chang nodded again, stuck on the first page of the Pretzel Connection paperwork: PLEASE READ THIS NOTICE. IT LIMITS OUR LIABILITY.

"Say it out loud, nice and clear."

"I understand," Chang said.

SOME NIGHTS HE COULD feel the anklet giving him spider kisses, seeping its antidote into his dreams, making him logy for the bus ride to work. Behind his Pretzel Connection station, a wall of brown butcher paper covered the glass entrance to an abandoned JCPenney. Chang would keep his back to this, uncomfortable with the darkness peeking out from behind the curled paper. At least a hundred feet of old tile stretched in front of him before the railing of the terrace. Past that, he saw rows of vacant retail space, some units shuttered with steel roll bars, some framed in streaked glass.

From this vantage point, he could see only one functioning business: Cutlery Connection. He'd spent his first two lunch breaks eating jalapeño pretzels and window-browsing the store's useless nostalgia—old gas station signs, rounded Betty Boop lunchboxes, tacky tin wall hangings of Princess Di and Madonna. Blazing track lights lit up the window's centerpiece, a beautiful collection of knives labeled, in flowing old-timey cursive, *the Mariner Collection*. In his past life, he used to wander through stores like this, fantasizing what he would buy everyone for Christmas if he had been compelled, by forces unknown, to shop at one store only.

Some days Pretzel Connection had no customers. When they did, it was always lone men, stragglers from the parking lot, oblivious to his animated shirt. On his fifth lunch break, Chang finally walked to the railing and peered over. The mall continued underground for at least twenty stories, maybe more; his eyes were bad. The dull roar he'd mistaken for air conditioning had been a distant river of shoppers.

On his second Wednesday of freedom, he was rereading his employee handbook, memorizing random paragraphs.

"Hello? Is anyone here?"

He looked up to see a small woman grasping the railing with one hand, leaning blankly toward the space he occupied.

"Yes. Right here."

"Do you sell pretzels?"

"Pretzels. I do sell pretzels."

"I know this is a long shot, but do you still carry the mango ones?"

He checked his clipboard, surprised to discover that he did indeed have a half dozen mango pretzels in the hold.

"Yes," he called out.

"Oh, good! Good! Keep talking and I'll walk to you."

He put his paper hat back on, feeling like a ghost.

"What do you want me to talk about?"

She smiled, producing a tiny silver cane and lightly tapping each tile once.

"That's good. Anything."

"Well, you're getting closer." He realized that her eyes were not still, but slowly moving, as if examining huge works of overhead sculpture.

"I just heard this morning that there was one of these pretzel carts on the top level, and I've been craving these all week. Even though I didn't want to get my hopes up."

"You work in the mall."

"At The Secret Garden. The bookstore. Not the lingerie place."

"I haven't been down that far yet."

She was close enough for the faint glow of his shirt to illuminate her features, like old neon.

"Really. Are you new here?"

"Yes. Second week."

"Ah! Well, allow me to officially welcome you to the southeastern corner of Heritage Park Mall. I'm Astrid." She offered a petite hand in his direction, the cane retracting into the other palm with a smooth mechanical motion. He realized she resembled an older, shorter Ingrid Bergman.

"I'm Chang."

She tilted her head. "Are you Asian?"

He caught himself for a moment, absorbed by that open face, releasing her hand.

"No. Ah, it's actually just…a typo. A nickname. From a typo. On my processing papers." He winced. "From when I was in the military." Her face went dark for the beat it took the shirt to switch its message to I AM NOT ALLOWED TO TALK TO CHILDREN.

"Oh, you were in the service! Which branch?"

He felt the need to swallow, glancing around for some third party to hold up a cue card, past the railing, over to the Cutlery Connection window, its bright row of knives.

"The marines."

"The marines! How exciting! Were you in Santiago?"

He gave one more look of helpless defeat to the knives.

"Um, well...I wasn't in those marines, ma'am." He laughed softly as blood pooled in his cheeks. Instead of frowning, she tilted her head upright and offered another curious smile.

"Mango pretzel?"

"Mango, of course."

He fumbled in the pushcart, the dim light from his shirt illuminating the neat cellophane wrappers of the wares. Looking up, he found a twenty-dollar bill carefully crimped into a delicate triangle, resting on his clipboard like a flag placed on a casket. She took the pretzel, eyes closed.

"I haven't had one of these in years."

He carefully unraveled the loose origami of her money.

"This is an interesting fold you have here, Astrid."

"That's how I tell," she said between bites, "which bills are which."

"But how do you know I'm giving you the correct change?"

She walked off a bit, hand out and receptive for the curve of the rail, chewing, thinking it over.

Finally, over her shoulder, Astrid said, "You have an honest face."

CHANG CLOSED UP THE cart at five the next afternoon and walked east along the empty mezzanine, toward the map Morton had mentioned. Several city blocks of unoccupied storefronts and empty wooden benches passed before he found the mounted chart standing aloof in public space, like a mighty plastic tombstone. Looking over its convoluted schematics, he understood that a much larger underground shopping mall connected all the old malls within five miles of each other. There must have been several thousand stores listed here.

The decision to engage had already been made for him; it felt less stressful to plunge in than to try to hide. A succession of escalators led him down into the bowels of a vast department store. He skirted the flow of blasé crowds, moving behind displays, always aware of the nearest exit. Promenades led to further unfamiliar sections, overlarge interiors filled with self-illuminated mannequins, perfume stands, wall-sized televisions, a region of lamps and ceiling fans and trellises and giant shoes. In the mirrored perimeter behind a wall of men's coats, he suddenly saw himself, a droopy nobody. Whatever menace had once lived in this person—this harmless little man with an honest face and a blinking shirt—had long since moved on to heartier hosts.

Down several escalators he found the beginnings of the shopping mall common area. Two levels below he understood why no one stared at his shirt. A group of loud teenagers came barreling out of a Spencer's Gifts. One gangly boy with a fuzzy mustache wore a shirt that blinked FUCK UP in alternating greens and reds. The girl next to him displayed a full pornographic movie playing on her chest. Farther along, he saw a bored middle-aged mother pushing a baby stroller in her own shirt reading SUCK MY FUCK, this one alternating between words and a short cartoon he didn't stare at. More whooping teenagers passed, each of their shirts trumpeting something crass, some rude word, or worse. No one cared.

At the edge of level six, a giant macaroni noodle framed the entrance to a descending escalator, the boundary of his terrain. He walked along the railing of this forbidden zone. The food court itself formed another terrace below. He thought of Secret Garden and, with a start, realized he could see the front of the store, just two floors down. He could see families laughing, bright displays of tall paperbacks and magazines. Chang thought of some piece of Greek mythology that began like this, someone gazing over the rim of a world they could never enter. Had they been watching from the heavens, or scowling down into the underworld?

ON WEEKENDS, HE WAS under house arrest. He wanted to spend both days sleeping, but a strange wakefulness took hold, the same tensing he'd undergone in the first months at Rahway State Prison. All Saturday afternoon and evening he watched TV in the quiet living room. The nameless old lady shuffled past around midnight, saying nothing. He hoped her room upstairs had a door. In the kitchen, preparing spaghetti, he found a stained, handwritten list buried in the utensils drawer, **RULES OF COMMUNAL LIVING**. He read this anxiously, finding that he had violated nothing, then tucking it carefully back under an oily spatula.

Later, watching a comedy with subplots and references that escaped him, Chang heard the front door slam. The man he'd seen earlier in his doorway walked past and doubled back.

"Hey."

"Hey," Chang said, rising from the couch. They shook hands in the middle of the living room, shirts warning both to protect their children from each other. The other man was younger than Chang, dull-eyed, with a grocery bag under one arm.

"You want a beer?"

"Oh. No. Thanks. I thought we weren't allowed out at night."

Shrugging, then turning toward the kitchen, the younger man asked, "Who can afford to check up on us these days?"

He returned with a beer and sat down. "You must be Sheldon. I'm Hector."

"Nice to finally meet you."

"Yeah."

Hector took the remote and switched to a soccer game.

"How many of us are there?" Chang asked.

Momentarily reading the scores, Hector grimaced, then said, "Who?"

"Us, here in the house. How many residents?"

"This is it, man," Hector said. "Lewis got hit by that car last month, so…yeah, we're it."

The soccer game eventually gave way to a commercial for a product he didn't recognize. Hector yawned and said, "You've got a letter around here somewhere."

Chang sagged into the arm of the couch, stunned. The younger man leaned over and rummaged through a pile in the corner, turning over phone books and encyclopedias. "Shit man…somewhere…"

"Do you remember," Chang said, hearing his voice as a dull whine, "who the letter was from?"

"Nah," said Hector, flipping through the pile on the shelf under the television. Finally standing, saying, "Nah. Nah. It's gone. Oh well."

"This is the worst time of year," Astrid said on Monday. "It's all seasonal, you know."

He handed over a papaya-cheesecake pretzel, saying, "Probably not up here it's not."

"That's right," she laughed. "You're immune to the tides of commerce."

She swallowed, then added, "I hear in the winter they have these enormous snowflakes hanging from the top floor. Just gigantic. I guess that would be up here somewhere. Twenty or thirty feet across, I'm told. It's a wonder they haven't killed someone."

"I suppose Christmas must be your big season."

"Oh no," Astrid said, turning to face him. "No, no. Next month. When school starts again. I mean, we're the second largest children's bookstore in north Jersey. It's a madhouse."

His stomach made a low groan. "I didn't know," Chang said flatly, "that you only sold children's books."

"Of course!" Her eyes sparkled a useless, decorative sea green. "You need to come and visit us!"

He stalked the upper concourse after work, remembering that he was a monster. A pair of elderly men eyed his torso hurriedly as they passed on their power-walks. He wondered what it must be like to grow old into this world, to have to watch the planet slowly sink into vulgarity, everything swirling down toward a lowest common denominator. When he reached the large mall map, marking his furthest point on this floor, he realized he had no idea where he was going.

A few shops could be seen further along. As he walked closer, his perspective unfurled store names: The Nip Of The Lash, Fudge Factor, Sophisticated Devices. These were the stragglers, businesses that had no place in the high-pressure depths of the mall proper. He stopped in front of Sophisticated Devices. In an old newspaper article he'd had passed to him recapping Freddie Bolson's death, he'd read that Freddie had erased incriminating photographs from the hard drive of his home computer. The police would only say that they had painstakingly recovered the incriminating material by use of "sophisticated devices."

Inside the store, folding tables held bins of old cell phones, watches, portable CD players, and dusty disposable cameras. At the back of the store, he found things only peripherally connected to the world of electronics: fish tanks, binoculars, phonograph needles, boxes of old compact discs and batteries. The middle-aged man behind the cash register acknowledged him with a polite nod.

What could he say to Astrid? Gathering a pile of dirty, blinking laundry in the center of his room later that night, he thought over polite phrasings, clarifications, excuses for why he could no longer be her pretzel vendor. The hallway outside his door crooked a menacing left into darkness past the stairs. He found the light switch and tottered past several desolate, doorless bedrooms with his arms full. Near the back of the house, he found a cramped, damp alcove with a stackable washer/dryer combo growing a skin of rust. Rahway had sent him into the world with fifty dollars, two trousers, four boxer briefs, eight socks, a thin windbreaker, and a cheap duffel bag printed with the blobby logo of the NJ Department of Corrections.

On the tag of a shirt, he read THIS GARMENT BELONGS TO THE TAXPAYERS OF UNION COUNTY DO NOT WASH. He stuffed the shirt into the drum of the washer anyway, remembered Morton's iron handshake, and dug it out in a dull rage. Rummaging on a plastic shelf for detergent, he found an envelope from the NJ DOC bearing his name.

He retrieved a check for $2,241 and a slip listing a few deductions he didn't understand. Chang leaned against the dryer and exhaled. He vaguely remembered, long ago, someone complaining from a neighboring cell about earning only eight cents an hour. They had been paid. He had pondered this occasionally at the end of an eight-hour shift in the clean, expansive U ward laundry hall, thinking of the day's sixty-four cents accruing in a distant bank account. He remembered nights when he'd floated off to sleep trying to work out the math.

"I'M BECOMING A REGULAR here."

He handed her the banana-chutney pretzel. "There are still a few flavors you haven't tried."

"Don't try to sell me on that nasty shrimp thing. I won't do it. What sort of drinks do you have?"

He listed off the sodas, wondering if she could see perfectly well, if she was some sort of spy send sent to monitor him.

"Are your other regulars as methodical as I am?"

"Ah…" He paused. "You should probably know something."

She seemed to scan the space between them, meeting his eyes and then drifting off. "Yes?"

"I'm not."

"You're not?"

He cleared his throat. "I, ah." He looked up to a louvered metal duct, far overhead, all that displaced air.

"I don't have any other regulars."

She laughed, eyes drifting again. "Good. They're a pain in the ass." He laughed, too, catching the slight waver in his own voice.

She finished a bite and said, "They are. All of 'em. The same mothers always whining about the fourth Hubert Hedgehog book when there's a great big poster near the cash register as big as can be—Denise told me—saying that we won't even be taking preorders until Labor Day. As if we had a secret stash in the back, you know? And creepy regulars, too. This one woman who keeps buying a copy of *Harry The Dirty Dog* every week. Isn't that strange?"

He nodded, then grunted to indicate the nod.

"And I hear things, too, you know. I mean…I pay attention to sounds more than most people." This was the first time she'd acknowledged her blindness. "You know, small things. Like this guy who comes in every day for story hour. I can tell by his sniffles. But he never says anything, no "hello." People shouldn't be ashamed to admit they like to hear children's tales, you know? It's so silly."

"Yeah."

Chang stared down at one tile.

"Maybe I'll come down for story hour one of these days. When is it?"

THAT NIGHT HE WOKE to the usual pinprick on his leg. Later, he dreamed he was back at his parents' house. He was in the kitchen, hauling clothes out of the refrigerator, trying to force the wet laundry into the freezer. "Hey, Dad," he yelled into the next room. "How do I work this?" But there was no answer. He found the living room empty. His parents had fled. On the hall table he saw an envelope with his name on it, something they'd left behind, some sort of warning he was terrified to open.

The next day, Chang opened a checking account on his lunch break and bought a pair of binoculars at Sophisticated Devices. When his shift ended at six he made his way down to the balcony by the giant macaroni noodle. He wasn't sure what he was looking for in Astrid's store, and he didn't see anything unusual. From his angle, one could only view the store's marquee and about a dozen feet into the space. But he knew this was the dozen feet he'd need to watch.

He came back the next day on his lunch break, spotting nothing unusual. On day three of the stakeout, he carefully read his employee handbook, discovering that his forty-five-minute lunch break could fall anywhere in the shift. He arrived at his balcony perch an hour early and spotted his quarry. A thin man in a red cardigan arrived at Secret Garden, took a magazine from a front rack, and opened it without reading. This would be story hour. Chang watched the man's face, recognizing an expression, an alertness. The man let his eyes stray off the printed page, scanning his vicinity without turning his head. Children drifted around this man, this stranger who moved about the width of the space, never venturing deep enough inside to be out of binocular range. It was one of the few riddles of life Chang knew the answer to. *You need to stay toward the front of the store*, he thought, *so you can make a quick exit.* He knew this routine.

THE NEXT DAY WAS Friday. He surveyed the lower levels for an hour after work, searching in vain, mindful not to miss the 7:20 bus. Riding the escalators up to the surface, he wondered what his options were. *Would mall security believe him? Would Astrid?*

He boarded the bus and found a space halfway in. With one fluid motion, Mr. Morton eased his huge body into the seat next to Chang and placed a giant steel hand on his thigh, pinning him in moving space.

"Mister Chanfield. I understand you've been watching children with a pair of binoculars."

He sat limp under this grip, helpless.

"Well?" Morton asked, inching his face closer to Chang's.

"They're in my duffel bag," he said quickly and quietly. "Take them."

Morton relaxed his grip and leaned back, sighing.

"Sheldon, Sheldon. I'm morose. Do you know why?"

He shook his head, miserable.

"Sheldon, I'm morose because it looks like you are a nice guy, you don't disrespect me, you always call in. But what it sounds like is that

I will eventually have to tear your ass in half. Now, doesn't that make you sad?"

"Yes," Chang whispered.

IN THE BATHROOM WITH no door, he jerked a brush across his teeth, the only exposed part of his skull. Inflation had warped the value of everything in this world, but not so badly he couldn't plot a course. The $2,200 could get him somewhere—get to New York, buy some new shirts, and catch a flight to Mexico, maybe.

He rinsed and spit into the stained sink. Sitting on the toilet, Chang pondered what he would do in Mexico, penniless, unskilled, knowing no Spanish. Maybe not Mexico then. The USA was big enough to lose himself in. Figure out some way he could get access to Depo-Lupron. Find a corner of the world where people were still civil, where he didn't have to see reflections of himself. Figure out how the world runs. Learn how to avoid detection for the rest of his life.

"Yo." He looked up to see Hector leaning in the doorway, eyes at half mast.

"You want a cream-cheese sandwich?"

Chang shook his head, wondering if he was supposed to acknowledge the invasion of privacy.

"Listen. Sheldon. I need to ask you something, and I need a straight answer. If I start up a neighborhood watch, are you in or out?"

In front of his stand, Astrid chewed her lip gently.

"I have a bad feeling about this."

"Your call," he said. "Yes or no?"

"Oooohhh. Hmm. What do you think?"

"Personally, I've never had the spicy strawberry shrimp." He rubbed his eyes, sleep deprived. "But then again, I'm not as adventurous as you, Astrid."

"You're not," she said, face brightening. "Good point. Hand it over."

"I would like to now formally apologize, on behalf of the Pretzel Connection company of Rochester, New York," he announced, "that there is no plaque to award you upon completion of all twelve flavors."

"I'll keep your name out of my angry letters."

The day before, he'd gone to Sophisticated Devices and bought a dusty laser pointer. The man behind the counter had rung him up while chuckling, saying only, "Trick or treat!" Even with Chang's bad eyes, the tall stranger had been easily visible in front of the Secret Garden.

Chang had waited for a moment to present itself. Next to the magazine rack, the man had crouched by a tiny boy.

All the rituals came back to Chang instantaneously, the astonishing ease of transferring trust. He aimed the laser pointer and fired. Two floors below, a small red dot appeared on the back of the man's head. Chang joggled the light, and it caught the attention of the little boy. His tiny hands went up, shielding his eyes. The tall stranger pivoted, looking around, and the boy stepped away, back into the gravity of a parent. The tall man had stood, also squinting, the dot playing off his face.

Chang hadn't intended to make himself known. He'd planned on scaring the guy, serving a warning shot. But the man had stood his ground and slowly surveyed the terrain, far from flustered. Chang pictured himself as he would be seen from below, only one blinking shirt among many. The man glanced up at the balcony and acknowledged his detection with a leering smile, a gesture of bold-faced defiance that made Chang bolt up escalators and out into the parking lot, panting for breath.

At the cart now, Astrid politely took a few bites of her pretzel, eyes open.

"So how come you haven't been to the bookstore yet?"

"How do you know I haven't?" He instantly regretted saying this.

She paused for a moment, registering a blankness that could be hurt.

"Which book," she finally asked, "did Denise read from yesterday?"

"Ah. Something about a talking tugboat, I forget exactly. Listen…I have some bad news. Today's my last day."

"What?"

"Yes," Chang said firmly. "I've been called up. To Barcelona. My entire division's going."

"That is absurd."

"It is absolutely absurd, and it is absolutely the truth. I leave at oh-six-hundred."

"Oh. I guess I really have graduated from the Pretzel Collection course."

"Connection."

"Connection, of course. Damn it, I'm sad, Chang."

"Me, too. You have no idea," he said, also regretting his phrasing on this.

"Well. Let me pay you then."

She handed over the folded rhombus that he knew was a ten-dollar bill.

"Please keep the tip. I have really enjoyed your company."

"Likewise."

"How long a flight do you have?"

"Long."

"Well. I'd give you a hug," she said, extending a hand, "but I guess we don't know each other well enough for that."

"We don't."

They shook hands.

He watched her seek out the railing, those eyes still examining grand, unseen works of art on the walls of an invisible cathedral. Then she rounded a corner and was gone.

Only today, on this last day of gainful employment, he finally got a dirty look. This was at Cutlery Connection. The old man who sold him the eight-inch Grand Mariner knife read his terrible T-shirt and looked at him through worn, watery eyes, saying, quietly, "Don't ever come back here."

Chang smiled. "I won't. Thank you."

Before the second escalator, he doubled back toward a small post office annex. In an old copy of the Yellow Pages, he'd found an ad for a children's hospital in Newark, some place with sad clip art suggesting they could use $2,200.

It took nearly twenty seconds for the escalator to descend to the next level. He worked out the math. Three and a half minutes minus forty seconds.

Chang reached the terrace that overlooked the food court. Story time would just be starting. He stood for a moment, watching the crowds, the flow of nonentities. Zipping up his windbreaker, he hoped it would be over quickly.

Sighing, Chang stepped through the giant macaroni.

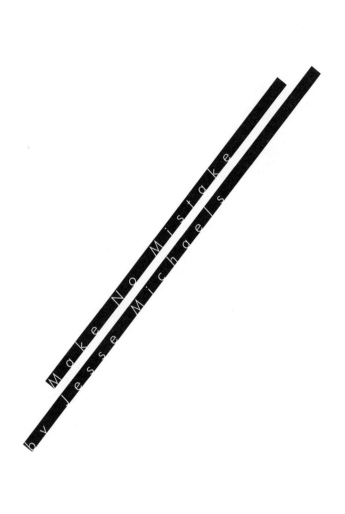

Make No Mistake

by Jesse Michaels

If you were with a friend at a party, and you saw your friend flirting with somebody who you knew was bad news, you might say something to your friend, something to warn him or her. On the other hand, you might just let it go. That is what you might call a *fulcrum* type of moment. If you will. I am saying, I call this kind of moment a *fulcrum* moment.

A *fulcrum* is a stick braced on a rock used to pry something—it multiplies leverage. In other words, a fulcrum moment is one where you can do a *small* thing, and have a possibly *large* effect—and if you don't do the thing, you'll probably regret it. Do you know what I mean? I am assuming you do because I think most of us recognize those moments.

Unfortunately, I think most of us recognize those fulcrum moments *after* the fact. *After* you let the person you should have talked to walk away, *after* you skipped the apology, *after* you decided *not* to stand up for yourself and just ate the insult. I mean those kind of *could-have/ should-have* fuck ups are the story of *my* life, maybe yours has been better. I hope so. But *this* is a story about how I got one of those fulcrum moments *right*. It's kind of a long story, but I promise you, every detail is necessary. So just wait. Or else skip it, I don't know.

It was 2007 or '08. Ish. I had been very depressed. I was living in San Francisco and drinking too much and a bit poor and fucked up. Back then you could live in the city even if you were poor. I was a normal young man, mid-twenties, maybe a little dog-eared. I was a real square. I didn't have any interests except that I liked to read. As a matter of fact, you might say I read obsessively. But not to any productive end. It was a painkiller. I had a little bit of money, not much. It was raining out. I was seeing a therapist. One day when I walked into the office there was a young woman in there.

She was about my age. She looked like a Cold War–era Russian-type dressed in clothes from secondhand stores. She was skinny and nervous. I wouldn't have been surprised if she was involved with pills or even "huffing." The waiting room was extremely small and our knees were almost touching once I sat down.

There was another therapist in the same suite. I assumed she was going to see him.

She shot a few skulking glances at me. I was reading *Mother and Baby* which was the only magazine to be found. The last week there had only been a ragged *Sports Illustrated*. I wondered what had happened to it and where this *Mother and Baby* had come from. She was just sitting there. I glanced down into her purse and noticed that there was a plastic sandwich bag inside with several partially-smoked cigarettes.

As we sat there, the little waiting room got clammy with human awkwardness. I tried to focus my attention on the article I was reading, which was about the differences in menopause between women who had or had not given birth, but it was hard to concentrate. Especially since she wasn't reading anything, she was just sitting there. Ten minutes passed in that waiting room. I realized that my therapist, Steve Belmick, wasn't going to come out to get me even though it was now almost a quarter past the hour. I couldn't take it anymore. I got up and knocked. There was no response. I opened one of the doors of his office, and then the other. Their offices have two doors back to back with each other for sound-proofing purposes.

My therapist Steve Belmick was face down on the floor of his office. His arms were by his side and he was breathing slowly and heavily. I had seen him doing this before. He was meditating. I could see part of one of his eyes and it was open. His head was red. I didn't know if it was wise to go in but I had opened the doors already so that was that.

As I was closing the outer door behind me, I heard the girl in the waiting room say, quietly but distinctly, "Fucking cock."

The last consonant was slightly cut off by the sound of the door shutting, but I was completely sure of what she had said. I walked into Belmick's office in confusion and alarm, going over the moment repeatedly. Could it be possible? It was shocking. There was no getting around what she had said and that it was directed towards me. Her tone of contempt confirmed it. Had I done something to offend her? Did I know this person? Belmick didn't react although I thought he probably heard it also. He didn't move his head. His face was pressed against the floor.

"Hi, Noah," he said, his voice compressed from the pressure on his face. "Sorry, I lost track of the time."

"Hi, Steve," I said. "Hey did you hear that? Did you hear what that girl out in the waiting room just said to me?"

"No."

"She just said, 'Fucking cock!' For no reason!"

Steve turned his head toward me. His face was indented with the weave of the carpet.

"Wow. Let's talk about it."

THE APPOINTMENT WAS PRETTY typical. We talked about the girl. He asked me how my week was. He tied the current information to larger patterns we had discussed before. He concluded with some possible behavioral ideas. I don't know. Therapy is therapy. I don't do it anymore, to tell you the truth. But back then I got something out of it. After the appointment I walked out of the office. She was still out there. She was chewing an enormous piece of gum in such a way that a small part of the gum would stick out of her mouth every third rotation or so. I could see that the gum was comprised of at least five pieces. I wondered for a second if I was making a mistake and that she was eating a piece of paper. An offensive letter? She looked up at me, chewing. Why was she still there? Hadn't her therapist come out to get her?

"Did you say something to me before I walked into that office?"

"Yes," she answered.

I stood there. I wasn't sure what to say next.

"Well, what was it?" I asked.

"I said, 'You fucking *rock*.'" The gum came out of her mouth and then tumbled back into it.

"Bullshit! You said, 'Fucking cock!' I heard you!'"

"I'm sorry, you must have the wrong person."

"The wrong person? How could I have the wrong person?"

"Look, what's your name?"

"Noah."

"This has all been a misunderstanding, Noah. I'm Mandy."

"Well, hello, I guess. I'm not sure why you ambushed me, but have a nice day." I started to walk out but then she spoke again.

"Oh well. We're off to a bad start, aren't we? What are you doing right now?"

"I'm going home. I just wanted to ask you what that was all about."

"What *what* was all about?"

"When you said, 'fucking cock.'"

She sighed and shook her head. "Is this how you pick up on girls? If it is, I'll tell you something...*I think it's working.*"

I started to walk out the door of the waiting room again.

"Do you know where the corner of Church and Market is?" she called after me.

"Huh?"

"Well, I'll be there at eight o'clock tonight, if you know what I mean."

"I don't know what you mean."

"Be there."

"I can't make it."

"*Be there,*" she repeated, this time with insinuation.

"Goodbye," I said, closing the door behind me.

I HAD NO INTENTION of showing up at the place that nutty girl had mentioned. I changed my mind by the time I got home, though. I just didn't have anything else going on. That night at around seven I walked toward Church and Market. I had a last moment of doubt—it wasn't too late to just turn around. But it didn't take. She was there on the corner with a cigarette and a green sun dress. She looked nice but skittish. She reminded me of a tortoise-shell cat that my uncle had when I was a kid that used to pounce on people from the top of cabinets.

"You know this is the Marpathala Yoga restaurant we're going to, don't you?" She asked me when I walked up to her.

"We're going to a restaurant?"

"A *Marpathala Yoga* restaurant."

"What's that?"

She shook her head in disbelief. "Marpathala Yoga is the type of yoga where they heat up the room while you're working out."

"Why do they do that?"

"Because it's amazing. You do the postures in a 130-degree studio. Every ten minutes a blast of steam comes in through the ceiling. It's absolutely fantastic. People sometimes vomit or pass out, but afterward every muscle in your body has been renewed. It's like running yourself through a washing machine or a garbage compactor or something. The last time I did it I solved a whole bunch of problems, and I mean *hard* ones."

I slowed down. "Wait a second, they heat up the restaurant? This sounds like a bad idea."

"No, it's great, Noah! It's a great way for us to get things cooking."

"No, this really sounds dangerous."

"It's the best thing you can do for yourself, and for *us*."

"What do you mean 'us'? We don't even know each other!"

"Oh, don't be naïve."

WE GOT TO THE restaurant, The Flaming Door. There was a lobby area with a desk and some attendants who handed us each a towel and a small cotton garment which they referred to as a "khafta."

"Have either of you eaten here before?" one of them asked.

"Oh, I have, but *he* hasn't," Mandy said. She said it as though she was telling him that I had never been to a doctor or read a book or something.

The attendant turned to me. He was very skinny and had sunken eyes.

"Okay, the first thing is to put on your khafta. You can leave your clothing in one of the lockers in the shower room. Once you get in the dining area, it's going to be *hot*. Now, it's okay if you need to drink water or lie down for a few minutes but we ask you not to leave the room for the duration of the meal."

Mandy and I went to separate shower/locker rooms and then met in the main dining area. The garment they had given us was toga shaped, but then it tapered off into a semi–loin cloth. It was humiliating but at least it was dimly lit in the restaurant. People sat at low tables talking. The heat was overwhelming, immediately. The waiters didn't seem to be affected; they weren't sweating and were moving around briskly, but the diners at the tables were red-faced and exhausted looking. They sat sighing in front of black plates with heaps of rice and vegetables on them. Once we sat down at our table Mandy produced a flask from inside her garment. She passed it to me under the table.

"Drink some of this; it will take the edge off."

As she said it a blast of steam shot into the room from a vent in the ceiling. People at the table next to us groaned and nodded to each other. A couple in the corner was eating soup. Sweat was dripping off of their faces into their bowls. I took a hit from the flask. I was expecting water but to my surprise it was gin. I passed it back to her.

"THIS IS CRAZY, MANDY; let's get out of here before it's too late."

"Well, we can if you want but I'll tell you this right now: you aren't going to solve your problems by lusting after comfort," she chided.

"I feel like I'm going to die!"

"Your challenge is that you don't know how to *let go*."

"No, it's just too hot! I let go of things all the time!"

"You only let go of the things that are easy to let go of. The little attachments that weren't that important anyway."

"You don't even know me! Who are you to say what I let go of?"

"Oh, I know your *type*. I do. From the minute I set eyes on you in that stinking little lobby at the therapist office."

I felt dizzy. "What type is that?"

"Oh, you know, the slick, womanizer type. Always looking for the next conquest. A fucking cock."

"See! You did say 'fucking cock'! I knew it!"

"Don't be ridiculous, I was just repeating what you *said* I said."

"Well, anyway, what do you mean 'womanizer'? What do you think I was doing in that therapist's office, looking for chicks? I'm antisocial; I haven't had a date in months."

"Oh, don't play that game with me! I can see exactly who you are, especially in this environment."

"Why especially in this environment? I can barely see across the table."

"Because it's *spiritual* in here!"

A waiter walked by with a pinched expression on his face. I had already finished my water and tried to flag him down for a refill.

"Excuse me!"

The waiter winced when he heard my voice and kept going.

"You have to call the waiters 'Baba' here!" Mandy said.

"Why should I call him Baba? I just want a glass of water."

"It's honorific. Waiters represent the divine in this restaurant, they're meant to be treated like gods. That's why they walk around with those little garden sprinklers."

As she said it I saw that the waiter who had blown me off was at the next table misting our neighbors with a little water sprayer he was carrying. The people smiled and thanked him.

"I don't understand. What does that water sprinkler have to do with him representing the divine?"

"He's raining."

I was really getting hot now. My "khafta" was soaked through with sweat and I was looking around at other tables to see if there was any leftover water I could grab.

"Baba, we pray for water?" Mandy whined the next time the waiter walked by. He gave us a disdainful look before filling our glasses.

"You'll have the broccoli and you'll have the vegetable Apavakana," he informed us.

After about ten minutes the food came. There was more sneering condescension from "Baba" and blasts of steam. The dishes were bland and undercooked but it really didn't matter; it was clear that the experience was meant to be more a test of endurance than a culinary event. The temperature of the room was punishing. After a short time I couldn't eat any more. For the first time, our waiter showed interest in us and hurried over to our table as soon as I pushed my plate away.

"Okay, I'm going to have to ask you to try and do a little better with that," he said.

"I really don't think I can eat anymore, I feel a little bit sick."

"Three more bites."

My eyes were stinging. I ate a little bit more while the waiter stood over me with his hands behind his back.

"I know it's not easy the first time but we all have to make a special effort," he said as he took my plate.

MANDY THANKED THE WAITER. After a little while we got the check and then went to our locker rooms. Outside in the lobby I noticed that as people emerged from the locker rooms and waited for their companions they smiled and nodded to one another knowingly. I sat there and smiled and nodded in case anybody was looking at me. Mandy showed up and we stepped outside. The night air was bracing in contrast to the room we had just been in. I felt like I had been boiled and rung out.

"Listen, Noah, do you want to come over to my house and watch TV or something?"

"I don't know, I feel a little nauseous."

"Oh, you should go back in! They have buckets for that."

"Forget it."

"Look, come over to my house and I'll make you some tea."

"All right, but no more heat."

We strolled down Church in the direction of Dolores Park. People were driving around looking for parking or else already on foot, headed for places where they could flee into noise, smoke, and each other. The night closed in. Steam rose from grates and a few cats crept around.

Her house was a small apartment in the Mission district. You went through a gate and then there was a driveway leading to a flat which was a converted basement. A white pit bull dogged around in the little enclosed driveway area. It followed us into the house shaking his tail violently so that his whole midsection swayed back and forth. That was the first night we spent together, and after that I ended up seeing her pretty regularly. She was wild, but kind of funny and not too hard on the eyes. I wasn't trying to find a wife or anything. To tell you the truth, I liked her.

TWO WEEKS LATER WE went to this Eritrean bar called Lazlo's over on Fillmore. The place was attached to a restaurant and wasn't even a freestanding bar of its own so there was never much excitement in there. We liked it for that reason. We got drinks. She drank gin and

I drank Scotch. The jukebox played looping, repetitive African music.

"Hey, by the way, what do you think of those In-N-Out hamburgers?" Mandy asked.

"No good," I said.

"What's wrong with you? Do you have to be different from everything?"

"I'd rather eat garbage."

"Go ahead! You'll never get along with anybody if you always feel you have to be different from everybody!"

"My therapist says I people-please too much."

"Who said that, Belmick?" she asked.

"Yeah."

"That reminds me, I think you should stop seeing that guy."

"What? Why?"

"I mean, it can have a negative effect. You sit there talking and talking and it's like being a baby in a stroller. And he's just pushing it around and around..."—she made a circling motion with her finger, and I noticed that her fingernail polish matched the lipstick—"...feeding you little pieces of fruit once in a while. That's why I quit seeing Pellman."

"Who is Pellman?"

"Oh, Pellman was my guy. He's in the adjoining office to your guy. That day I met you was supposed to be my last session with him but he didn't even show up. That shows you how much these people really give a shit."

"That's a really aggressive logical jump," I said.

"Huh?"

"You go from your therapist not showing up to all therapists not giving a shit. What the fuck is that?"

"Whatever," she said.

"Well, it just so happens that I am going to stop seeing Belmick. But not because you say I should."

"Really?"

"Yeah, I've already cancelled my next appointment."

"Why?"

"Well, I went in there because I was having a lot of trouble with the basic actions. You know, the basic moves. But now they seem to be coming to me."

"They are?"

"Yeah—I can make breakfast, form plans, return phone calls—you know, I'm back in the world of action."

"I'm so happy for you!"

She leaned over to me and threw her leg over mine and gave me a lurid hug. We were both getting drunk. We spent another hour in there and then took a cab back to her house where we drank and acted foolishly until late at night. Then she fell asleep. I stayed awake for a while with my arms around her. I felt lucky.

IT WAS ABOUT FOUR days after that night at Lazlo's (the bar). I hadn't seen Mandy for a couple of days. She hadn't returned my phone calls. One tries not to worry about the little slights in the beginning but one always fails.

Things were looking up in general. I had started taking a couple of classes. It can change that quickly sometimes. I mean your mood. I guess that even though I liked to think of myself as some kind of lone wolf, Mandy helped my morale considerably. That day I was arriving home from City College. I got my mail out of the box and went upstairs to my little egg of an apartment. There was a letter with no return address on it. I opened it.

*Noah—It's Mandy. Identity confirmation: I met you in a waiting room at the therapist's office. I will be gone for a few das* [sic]. *Maybe more. Could you please feed the dog, Bubbles, for a couple of days? You know where the extra key is. The food is under the sink. Don't worry or get weird about this. Think of Bubbles and do it. Please confirm the feeding of the dog by putting the fern that you have in your kitchen in front of the living room window. I will see the fern from outside and know that you have accepted this arrangement. Move the piece of fern around each time because I will be coming by every day to check. Important.*

The "identity confirmation" in the letter was unnecessary because Mandy's handwriting was unmistakable. It consisted of large, wildly written characters and was littered with smudges and red thumbprints. The thumbprints were caused by the fact that she pressed her left thumb against her lower lip while she was writing, blotting it with lipstick, and then clutched the page with both hands to read her work back. I had seen her writing things down before, it was a violent process.

I put the letter down and made coffee. I added milk and dropped a couple ice cubes in it and drank it quickly. Then I put a jacket on and walked out the door. I thought I may as well go and feed Bubbles while I had energy. She was a bit strange; who knew what was going on? I didn't understand the fern-in-the-window signal or why she didn't just call instead of sending a letter, but she probably had some reason for it.

Bubbles was thrilled to see me. I fed him. He had a little fenced-in enclosure to run around in but I took him for a walk anyway. The dog loped along in that intrepid way they have, sniffing everything. He was very strong but also aware of the tandem so that he never dragged me. A sensitive soul. We finished up the walk and I left Bubbles inside the fenced area. When I got home I moved the fern from my kitchen over to the living room window. I looked up and down the street to see if I could spot her hiding behind a mailbox or something.

A COUPLE OF DAYS later another letter arrived from Mandy. I was beginning to miss her and to wonder about her feelings for me. The letter was written in her usual thrashing script.

*Noah,*

*Please continue to feed and walk the dog Bubbles. I am surprised that you haven't tried*

*to find me. I guess that our relationship means
or doesn't mean something different from what
I thought it meant. If you think about it, how I
went to Berkeley last Friday to the Relaxation
Synthesis workshop, it wouldn't be too hard to
figure out that that was the last time you spoke
to me. I mean if it mattered to you. I suppose
it's beyond you to ask around or anything.
Have you tried to figure it out (where I am)? If
you have, DON'T. I am doing something pretty
important (maybe it wouldn't be important
to YOU, I don't really know at this point).
Anyway, don't think about any of this. I will
look for the fern at four o'clock.*

    *Sincerely,*

    *Amanda Percival*

I threw the letter away. I had already walked
and fed the dog that day as I had done twice
every day since I received her first letter. I had
also been moving the fern around the window
back at my house after each feeding, like an
idiot. Her formal closing hurt my feelings.
What had happened to the warmth I felt that
night we hung out at Lazlo's? Had it just been
a fuzzy illusion created by African guitar and
Scotch? I decided that I would wait by the

window and confront her when she came by to look for the signal. She had been gone for a week now. I had to put a stop to this. At around ten of four I started looking for her. I set my chair up so that I had a view of the street but I was more or less out of sight.

Time passed. I lived on a fairly inactive street. Like all of San Francisco, there was not a single parking space and yet few people seemed to be walking to or from the hundreds of cars. The light reflected off the windshields of the parked vehicles abrasively. One person walked by drinking from a cup with a straw. A cat looked up at the birds on the telephone wires and a man in a building across the street talked on a phone. A couple of cars went by. Then at around 4:15 or so a car drove by slowly. It was a beat-up red Sedan of some kind. Sure enough, there was Mandy, in one of the passenger seats. The car had other people in it. I could only make one of them out clearly—the young woman in the driver's seat. I didn't know what to do. I hadn't expected Mandy to be in a car. She had very few friends and she always walked everywhere. All the people in the car, including Mandy, were wearing sunglasses. I threw open the window quickly.

"Mandy!"

The car sped up. She must have seen me, or at least heard me, but she didn't indicate it. She just turned away nonchalantly as the car went to the end of the block and around a corner. I paced around the room. Had she been kidnapped? The people in the car looked fairly normal as far as I could tell or at least not like kidnappers, whatever kidnappers looked like. No, it was a voluntary situation. I retrieved the letter from the garbage. *If you think about it, how I went to Berkeley last Friday to the Relaxation Synthesis Workshop, it wouldn't be too hard to figure out that that was the last time you saw me.* It was Friday that day. She seemed to be hinting in the letter that I should retrace her steps. It was a strange little game. I supposed that I could just blow her off but I didn't want to. I remembered that the place she went to was a spa on College Avenue over in Berkeley. I knew where the place was.

At the BART train station in Berkeley a saxophone player blew improvisations under the enormous overpass. The tracks above formed a cavernous enclosure of gray cement and people bustled around below. The place reminded me of what I imagined Eastern Europe to look like—a lot of concrete and bustling around and aggressive jazz. As I walked by the horn player I winced. When he saw my expression he took a few steps toward me and looked at me dolefully, pretending that he was going to serenade me down the street. *Not bad*, I thought.

The workshop was in the back of the spa. There was a hallway which had doors to the right and left. Each door had some kind of symbol on it—a half moon, a seashell, a winged woman emerging from an egg—these were the treatment rooms. At the end of the hall there was a small conference room with about twenty chairs in it arranged in a circle. I chose a chair and watched as people showed up, looking for Mandy. She wasn't there. The words "Relaxation Synthesis" were written on a dry-erase board.

The facilitator was a curly-haired woman with jangling earrings and a sonorous voice. Once the room was filled she addressed the group.

"The difference between relaxation and Relaxation Synthesis is that relaxation is like drinking a glass of water while Relaxation Synthesis is like going so deeply into the well that we have enough water for the whole week." Many of the people in the room laughed knowingly. It was an easy crowd.

I didn't understand what the joke was. "For some of us, it's easier than for others," the instructor continued. This really got a big laugh and also some empathetic humming noises.

"This lady is really bringing down the house," I said to the man next to me. He smiled at me blankly.

After the preamble the woman led us into a guided trance state.

"Mmmmm…" somebody next to me moaned.

"…Now find your spirit guide. It could be a beloved teacher, a religious figure, or even a just a feeling-tone."

My eyes were lead balls sinking into the clay of the inner skull. I saw my (ex-) therapist, Steve Belmick. The strange thing was that, in my imagination, he was in a sauna and completely naked. I tried to get a towel on him mentally but it seemed like the harder I tried the more detailed his nakedness became. Now he was shining with sweat.

*This can't be right*, I thought.

"Whatever you see, go with it, even if it surprises you."

In my mind, Belmick nodded and waved. He had an erection.

When the lights came on, people milled around and chatted. I asked the teacher if she had seen Mandy but she told me that it had been a different facilitator the previous week. I was tempted to ask people in the class but I realized it would look like I was stalking somebody.

In the hallway on the way out a young woman with red hair came up to me. She was wearing a long dress and had a middle-American look, like she had just wandered in from the prairie or something.

"Did you like it?"

"It was great."

"I'm Heliotrope," she said.

"Noah."

"This kind of relaxation is a wonderful start, isn't it?"

"A start?"

"Yes—a way to get going. You know, kind of like turning the key to get the motor started."

"Oh yeah, I suppose so."

"Listen, do you need a ride somewhere?"

"Well, I'm going over to catch the BART train, actually."

"I would be happy to give you a ride!"

"Thanks, are you sure? I mean, I could easily just walk over there."

"Oh absolutely! I would love to do it."

We walked outside and got in her car. The station was only a few blocks away but I was feeling a little groggy from all the relaxation and I was glad for the ride.

"Do you mind if I stop somewhere on the way?" she asked.

"No, go ahead."

She turned off of College Avenue and onto a side street that wove upwards towards the Berkeley Hills.

"So, what do you do in your misery-life Noah?"

"My what?"

"Yes, you know, your misery-life. Your life in the outside world."

"Outside world? Outside of what?"

In response to my question she let out a peel of shrill laughter that verged on screaming.

"What's so funny?"

"Oh, nothing! I forget sometimes that people are so caught up in the big shred-mill!"

"What?"

She smiled stiffly. She was driving up into the hills, making no sign of stopping anywhere.

"Where are you going?" I asked.

"Huh?"

"Where are you going?"

"What?"

I let it go. I was getting a little bit scared. I kept my eyes on her while I felt around in the door compartment for a pen or something that I could fashion a weapon out of if I had to.

"So you're a student?" she asked.

"Uhh...yes. Well, I mean I'm taking a couple of English classes. How did you guess that?"

"Oh, English! I totally have hands for that!"

"Oh."

"Language is so important for getting past language!"

"Yes, that's my goal." I found a discarded popsicle stick in the crack of the car-seat. Useless, unless I could find some way to sharpen it.

Conversation ceased as she drove farther and farther into the hills. Finally she pulled up outside a large Victorian house. The yard was overgrown and the paint on the house was peeling off.

"We're here!" she shouted.

"Where?"

"Would you like to come in?"

"No, thanks."

"Listen, Noah, I don't mean to be forward. But I know you enjoyed that relaxation class. And this...well this could be what you are really looking for. Also, your friend is here!"

I stared at her in shock in the darkness of the parked car. This lady with the dress knew who I was all along. Mandy was obviously involved with this kooky woman and her big dilapidated house and now I seemed to be getting drawn in. It irritated me that all that Mandy had to do was write a vague letter and here I was. Was I that easy to manipulate? Obviously, yes. I sighed and opened the car door. In spite of everything, I was looking forward to seeing Mandy. As we walked up the steps to the porch, I realized that Nancy's car was the same red sedan I had seen cruising outside of my apartment with Mandy in it.

"Don't worry, Noah!" Nancy reassured. "You are exactly the kind of guy who is ready for the transmission!

We walked into the house. She led me into the living room. There was a group of about twenty people in there. The room was filled with collapsible chairs, all facing an open area on one side. The group of people consisted of men and women between the ages of twenty-five and fifty or so. I spotted Mandy quickly. She was wearing a long dress like Nancy. I walked over to her.

"Mandy, what is this shit? What's going on?"

"Noah, I have arrived at a transmission space. You have chosen to become part of this."

"A transmission space?"

"Yes. We have a leader now and some important purposes. I have come here tonight to get you to remember your true identity."

"What do you mean 'I have come here'? You were already here!"

"Noah, I'm talking in terms of your world picture, your misery-world event."

"I know, but even in my world-picture you were already here. I came here and found you."

"Your old analytical approach won't help you to get the transmission, friend."

"'Friend?' What the fuck? Have these people drugged you?"

"Only if Truth is a drug."

A couple of other people came up to us. They stood very close.

"Oh is this the man you were embroiled with on the misery-plane?!" observed a fellow in his thirties. He had a healthy look about him. Most of the others didn't look so hot.

"Yes," said Mandy.

"Mandy, I think we should leave."

"Oh, her name isn't 'Mandy' anymore."

I turned to Mandy. She was nodding.

"It's Perserverance," the man said.

"That's stupid," I said.

"Oh, that's the amazing thing about this—how 'stupid' turns into 'perfect' here!" said a woman standing two inches from me. She had dust-colored hair and filmy glasses.

The group of people around Mandy and I was growing. Soon I couldn't see beyond the circle of people pressing in around us. It was hot and everybody's face looked tired and oily.

"Why are you all standing so close?"

Everybody in the group laughed too enthusiastically. Mandy also laughed.

"Remember everybody? How it was? Before?" a man shouted.

"How YOU were you mean, Harvest!" answered a woman in a long dress.

"Oh, I think YOU were that way too, Trajectory!" the man kidded back. The room erupted in riotous laughter.

"The wonderful thing is that we can finally admit that we were ALL that way!"

Heliotrope said. The hot circle of people broke into a round of applause.

"Just listen to Him talk. You'll see what this is all about." Mandy said.

"Him? Who's 'Him'?" I asked.

The healthy-looking man who had first butted in leaned in between Mandy and I and covered his mouth with his hand as if telling me a secret. He was wearing a nylon track suit.

"Watch out! You might just UNLEARN something!"

"Oh ha ha! Ha ha!" a woman near him tittered.

At that moment a voice from outside the huddle announced that "the transmission is going to begin." I felt nauseous and dizzy. Several people led Mandy away from me. The healthy-looking fellow took me by the arm. "Couples who were embroiled before they got here are kept separate. My name is Filament," he said and patted me on the back of my head.

Everybody sat down in the chairs. I was given a seat near the front. Heliotrope, the woman who had lured me there in the first place, sat next to me and smiled at me intently every once in a while. My new friend

Filament sat on the other side. I noticed that Filament and Heliotrope kept staring at one another.

"Do you two want to sit next to each other?" I asked.

"Oh no!" said Heliotrope, embarrassed. "We're bookending you."

Filament smiled and nodded.

Once everybody was seated, the room quieted down. After a few moments I heard a humming noise. I realized that everybody in the room was humming a single tone. The group tone created a mesmerizing collective idiocy. I unconsciously started to hum right along with them but I stopped myself. I took a quick look around to see if I could spot Mandy but they must have buried her in the back somewhere. The crowd was normal looking, like everybody else in the world, but more child-like.

A door towards the rear of the living room opened. A man walked in wearing a frayed red bathrobe. The man was short and slender. He had a large mess of black hair and wore sunglasses. He was unshaven and walked slowly. He was about forty-five or so. People kept humming, but now the buzz was punctuated with loud exclamations from people around the room.

"Miller!"

"It's Miller! The one that solves disease!"

"Miller! We want the transmission!"

"Step near us walking man!"

"Write the book, big friend!"

"We're nothing but shit! Help!"

Miller stood in the cleared area at the front of the room and waited until the shouting died down. Once it was silent he waited a while longer. His sunglasses were totally black. He kept his gaze directed to the far distance. When he began speaking his voice was quiet and droning but was audible in the vacuum of people straining to hear. He started as though in the middle of a discourse rather than at the beginning.

"So, when you have a problem, you have to actually realize that the problem has the problem. That's why I'm here."

He paused. The pause went on for a long time.

Finally, he said, "I'm the Real Meal."

"Thank you, teacher!" somebody shouted.

"Let me explain: all the problems are over when you realize that the solution is the absence of the problem. I'm like the big absence. A lot of you came here with relationships. Here, we say that you were embroiled in relationships.

That means you were being broiled. The thing about being broiled is that when you're well done, you're dead."

Everybody in the room was transfixed.

"Some of you came here with money or maybe with no money. I eat all of it. I eat your 'have' and I eat your 'have-not.' I'm the Big Void. Look, I don't want to convince you of anything. What I'm trying to do here is unconvince you of things that you never really believed in the first place. It's called *unlearning*. You're going to find out that things can come out of your own mind which are pretty golden. You just have to get rid of the lead. What do you think they mean by 'get the lead out'?"

"Miller, we don't know!" an overweight woman with a headband whined. Other people in the room shrugged and laughed.

"They mean that you should get moving! Let me ask you this: Have you ever tried to move when you're bogged down with a thousand pounds of garbage? I'm the psychic garbage man. I don't claim to be or to do anything. This isn't about Miller. This is about the fact that Miller doesn't exist. That's why I can eat your garbage. I'm the Nothing Man. Your problem is that you exist too much. And I'm not saying you have a problem. You are a problem. Lay it down right here, friends."

He stood totally still. He gestured with his hand while he spoke. There was no movement in his wrist so that the arm-hand moved stiffly as if it were a single apparatus. It was weird but compelling.

"Friends, and I mean friends, I am not here to lecture you. You are here to avoid being nowhere. Look, look at TIME. All day long you plod and plot. Let me say something: get your feet out of the toilet and start walking the big circle! Need instructions? I don't have any. What I do have is a way for you to get free of your own disease. I solve disease by doing something with your fixation. The thing I do is unfix it. If it's not broken, don't fix it, right? But if it's not fixed, you don't have to worry about it breaking in the first place."

"Aaaaaah," responded the group.

"Society is playing a big game with you people. I'm like the referee with an empty rulebook. Can you understand that? I give you new names but all I'm really doing is letting you put your hands in the cake and see if you're still hungry. Of course you're going to feel hungry if you're looking in the window at all those cakes!" he shouted angrily.

A dark-complexioned man sitting in the same row as me had tears in his eyes.

"People, all I'm trying to do is take your eyes off the goddamned cakes!" Miller pleaded. He went cold again: "Let's start from the beginning. Slavery is over. But unless you know that you were a slave in the first place, you can't get that it's over. This is the transmission. This is the whole Transmission."

The talk went on for two hours. Miller talked about having your feet in the toilet and outer space and how cars drove people around and how the biggest enemy of all was bread. He covered a lot of ground. I went into a daze after a while. The man had unbelievable stamina. Finally, at around midnight he opened up the floor for questions. I was nodding off. Filament kept putting his hand on my shoulder and nodding. "You're doing great," he reassured.

"Miller," shouted a black woman near the back of the room, "Why is it that people don't understand us?"

"Thank you, Emergency. When I named you Emergency, it was because you EMERGE-AND-SEE. Let me explain something. The big problem with people is that they DO understand us. You see? We're the ones who DON'T understand. That's why we are free of disease. As long as they keep UNDERSTANDING, they are riding on the misery boat. When we got free of our misery-lives we didn't need to 'understand' anymore, we just do what we do while they don't what they don't."

"Miller," asked somebody else, "are you God?" People around the room laughed.

"Yes. Is that what you want me to say? No. No, no, no, no. YES! Right? That's the game we keep playing. What's God? Who's God? Are you God? Hmmm!" He acted out his perplexity by scratching his head and looking upwards.

"Miller, you're a dazzler, a real Merlin— how did you come to be so wondrous?" This woman was bleary-eyed and in her fifties. She was wearing a long flowered dress and seemed optimistic in a way that was outdated. She looked like a veteran of many craft fairs.

"Remind me of this woman's new name?" Miller asked the group.

"I love how human he is!" a man behind me whispered.

"You named her 'Bitch,' Miller," somebody reminded him.

"Oh yes. Bitch, I am wondrous because I am willing to dispense with the sludge and misery of mundane life. That's what God is. God is dispensing."

It went on and on. After a while I just started getting angry. Every time my head dipped into sleep and I had to haul it back up I became angrier. All the questions had resolved into talk about God. Finally, I decided to ask something myself, if only to stay awake. But I was delirious now and didn't even know what to say.

"I don't believe in God!" I shouted mindlessly. The room went silent as Miller turned toward me.

"Name him! Give him a new name!"

"Miller! We accept him!"

"Say it again, friend," said Miller.

"I don't believe in God!" I said, this time less defiantly.

"The God you don't believe in isn't the one I'm worried about."

Everybody in the room applauded. Filament massaged my shoulder.

"Welcome, New Friend. We'll call you 'Refund,'" Miller said.

"Refund! Refund!" the group shouted. Several people came over and touched me warmly.

AFTER THAT IT WAS time to go to sleep. Miller left the room unceremoniously and everybody went off to different parts of the house. I saw Mandy leaving with Heliotrope. I started to go over there but Filament took me by the arm and led me down a different hallway and up some stairs. There were several bedrooms along the hallway upstairs. All the doors had been removed from the bedrooms.

"We function as a single organ," Filament explained.

In the bedroom there were two small cots. I sat on one. It was too late to catch the train back to the city and I didn't want to leave until I talked to Mandy.

Filament undressed. He looked like a swimmer, a triathelete.

"I was a physical education major over at UC Berkeley until I met Miller," Filament said. "The transmission has changed all of that. I can see you are starting to pick up Miller's glow."

"I wouldn't say that."

"I'm going to be your Launch Friend. I'll be with you for the first couple weeks."

"My Launch Friend?"

"Yes. Yes. Yes."

"What's that?"

"Somebody to help you avoid logic."

"Why? Why would you want to avoid logic?"

"Miller would say that your question is eating it's own answer."

"What would you say?"

Instead of answering, Filament puffed out his cheeks and pantomimed chewing. Then he smiled and squeezed my shoulder.

I lay down. He turned off the light. The hours of weird talk had turned all my thoughts into rivulets of flowing mud. I lay there in the mud. Filament went to sleep instantly. I fell asleep after a while and dreamed of Miller talking and talking. In my dream I thought to myself, *Well there* is *something about him…*

I woke up after a couple of hours. Renewed by sleep I had less patience for it all.

"Filament?"

"Yes, Refund?"

"Please don't call me that. Listen, I need to talk to Mandy."

"Refund, it's very important that the two of you DON'T talk."

"Look, I really need to talk to her. After that, we won't talk."

"Look, it's critical that you two DON'T talk."

"I just want to ask her a couple things about what's going on here."

"Hey, it's kind of important that the two of you actually DON'T talk," he said soothingly. We lay back down. I remembered him and Heliotrope staring at one another.

"Listen, Filament, I noticed her leaving the room with Heliotrope. Is Heliotrope Mandy's 'Launch Friend'?"

"Yes."

"Well listen, maybe I could go talk to Mandy and you could talk to Heliotrope?"

"Well, they actually say that there shouldn't be a lot of talk in that way."

"I know but maybe you could talk to her and I could talk to Mandy and then that would be it. After that, no talk. No more talk."

After a few minutes I convinced him of it. People will always find a way to agree with what they actually want to do.

Filament led me down the hall and down the steps. The floorboards creaked. We had to go very slowly because it was noisy and there were no doors on the bedrooms. We crept through the house and down the stairs. Finally we got to the room we wanted.

Mandy was in there with Heliotrope. Filament went over and woke Heliotrope up. I woke Mandy up.

"Mandy, wake up! I'm here!"

"Noah?"

"Yes!"

"Noah?"

"Yes."

"Noah?"

"Stop it."

"Sorry, I don't understand why you're down here."

"Wake up."

"I'm awake."

"Look, Mandy, what is this shit? Let's get out of here."

"No, wait, you have to hear more about it."

"Why?"

"Miller has a plan."

"What is it?"

"You have to listen."

"I listened tonight. He was making me go crazy. Although I admit there's something about him."

"Do you like it?"

"No."

"Give it a shot, Noah."

"This is a cult."

"See? You're always making blunk statements like that. You're always painting everything with one brush and making a big blunk statement."

"It's not a 'blunk' statement, it's just how it looks to me. Who is going to feed your dog now?"

"My landlord is doing it. I got her to do it after I sent you the last letter."

"Listen, since you were going to San Francisco anyway to watch me move my fern around in front of my window, why didn't you just feed the dog yourself?"

"They are trying to disembroil me from my apartment. It was all I could do to get them to let me go back to the city to make sure you were taking care of him. I insisted on it though. Actually, there was a big meeting about it. I told them I was going to get out of here if they wouldn't at least let me make sure you were feeding Bubbles. Then they had a big meeting that lasted two hours. I was just about to walk out and then Miller said I could make sure you were doing it. I think they will probably just let me go get him in a day or two."

"Oh."

"I knew you would come find us!" she said and hugged me. "They wouldn't let me call you so I put it in code in the last letter. Heliotrope is my friend. She said she would get you up here if I could get you to the spa. That relaxation seminar is where they scout out candidates."

"Well this place bothers me."

"Oh, because some of the people are stupid?"

"No, it's not that. I lived in a big house like this for a couple of years when I was going to school. Not far from here, actually."

"You didn't like it?"

"No. My parents took care of the house for somebody. They were both addicted to pills. I read books all day."

"Wow, Noah! You never told me about that!"

"Well, there you have it."

Filament and Heliotrope were making out and groping each other over on the other cot. There was a lot of gasping and grabbing.

"Jesus!"

"I know!" Mandy replied.

"Look, Mandy, I'm going to listen to one more of these transmissions and then I'm going to get the fuck out of here! I've got a class on Monday, I don't have time for this shit."

"But you are going to listen to one more? That's great!"

"I don't know if it's great."

"It's great!"

We embraced and kissed. Any intimacy was destroyed by the mouthy noises of Filament and Heliotrope.

"Noah, you better go! I think if they keep at it they are going to try and fuck each other!"

"You got that right."

"Look, you really shouldn't be caught down here!"

"Okay."

I pried Filament off of Heliotrope. He was still panting as we snuck back.

THE NEXT DAY EVERYBODY gathered in the living room. They were all very excited because there was going to be a rare morning transmission. Again, I was kept separate from Mandy. Talking was discouraged. Rice was served in colored plastic bowls that had done too many dishwasher tours. Then it all began.

Everybody started humming. Miller emerged: bathrobe, hair, unshaven face, and opaque black sunglasses. The humming turned into shouting. He was disheveled, as he had been yesterday.

"Here comes the avatar!"

"Let us have it!"

"You are the only man alive!"

"Give us some knowledge-words!"

"We're hungry!"

Miller stood in front of the assembled group. The shouting ceased. Then he started as though he had already been talking like he did the night before.

"...AND SO WHEN I say that all the men here are homosexual, I mean that all of them are except for me. And the reasons should be obvious. You women here have finally found the straight man, the straight arrow. And that man is not to be found on a movie screen. This is the movie screen right here. Understand?"

"OH YES!"

"Look—people are very concerned about saints. Let me tell you something: every one of you here has a chance to be a saint, understand? It's no big deal. Once you get the transmission that I'm talking about, you are going to be just like Saint Francis, Saint Jerome, Saint Johnny Carson, Saint Adolph Hitler—you are going to be the one on the headlines. Why? Because you will have gotten rid of the newspaper. When you get rid of the stage, guess what? You're the star of the show. And I'm the one who gets rid of it. Not for you. I don't do anything for you. I do it underneath you. See, I'm the doormat and the umbrella at the same time. I'm the dirt on the sole of your shoe but I'm also the big blue atmosphere.

"The trick is, first your name has to go up in flame. Once you get rid of your name then you can really get a life that's on the edge. Listen, we can do this right now. Who wants to do this right now? Who is ready for the new world?"

"WE ARE, MILLER!"

"MILLER, WE WANT TO DO IT!"

One of the women in the group walked up to Miller with an enormous newsprint sketchpad and a pen. Miller took a page out of the pad and taped it to the wall.

"Who is first? Who is going first?"

"I will!" shouted a curly-haired fellow with an alpaca sweater.

"Okay, friend, tell me your name. No, not the name I gave you. Tell me your OLD name, your misery name, we're going to get rid of it altogether."

"My name is Ed Petri."

"Your name WAS Ed Petri!"

Miller wrote the name on the giant sheet of paper which was taped to the wall. ED PETRI. Then he produced a lighter and set the sheet on fire. The paper scorched the wall, sending lines of soot up towards the ceiling. Ed Petri's head rolled around as the paper burned as if he were receiving visions. Miller looked on from behind the sunglasses.

"That's it! That's all there is to it. You see how easy it is? Who's next?"

Somebody else volunteered. Miller taped another page in the same place on the wall. The process went on for twenty minutes. Miller burned page after page until a large section of the plaster was a blackened smear and the floor was covered with soot and ashes. People all over the room were rolling their heads around and going into delirium as their misery-names were torched. The room was now totally filled with smoke. My throat burned.

"I can't breath!" said a man near me who had not yet volunteered to have his name burned. The man had been hacking and coughing for the last ten minutes. Miller pounced on him.

"Vellum, Orbit!" Miller shouted to two men sitting near the front row. They got out of their seats. One was in his forties and balding and the other was younger with short, sweaty arms and blue sandals. They were larger and stupider than the other men in the room. (*Commune cops*, I thought.) "Take this asshole to the Orange Room! On the maximum!"

I thought there would be some protest from the coughing man but instead he lit up. "Thank you, Miller!" The two guys Miller had spoken to took the offender by the arms and led him out of the living room.

"You see you have to let go here, people. You have to give it all up and take a good look outside of the fish pond. Don't be tricked by smoke. Your parents are smoke. Your wives and husbands are smoke. You see? You have to flush it all away. Even PETS," He said with a stiff armed wave.

"Wait a second Miller—PETS?" came a familiar voice. It was Mandy.

The interruption caused Miller to pause. Then he kept right on rolling.

"All I'm saying, Perseverance, is we have to get disembroiled from the past. You see, a pet is a good friend but let me ask you this—who is feeding who? Who is wearing the collar? Who has fleas? You or the cat? You or the frog? Are we animals? Are they people? Maybe they are. But how are we going to know for sure if we are down there with them eating bugs?"

"Well MY DOG doesn't know about any of this!"

"Let me tell you a story. I had a dog once. The dog was a Doberman. He had a name. I had a name. Every day we walked around with our names. That's the problem. I traded him in for the transmission."

"You traded your dog?" Mandy shouted.

At this note, the people in the room started coming out of their name-burning reveries and paying attention to the goings-on. Miller took a quick glance at where the two guys who dealt with the last incident had been sitting. Presumably they were still in the Orange Room. Nothing happened for a few seconds. A couple of ashes drifted from the wall to the floor.

"Look—we all have Dross. Dross is what sticks to the skin even after the flaming up of Truth. What you have to do is decide what you want to do with it. Do you want to eat it?

"Do you want to sleep with it around your neck? Dross? Let me tell you a story. There was a fellow early in the transmission. We'll call him Ned Deasley. But I called him Decent Mineral. Anyway, he had this picture of his family he used to like to carry around. Now, listen. I have nothing against the family. It's just that we are here to plunge the bowl, you know?" Miller looked around the room. The people responded with a few *oohs* and *ahs* and somebody shouted, "Tell us more about it, More-teller!"

"Anyway, every time we turned around he would have this picture of his parents and his brother standing in front of palm trees and wearing polo shirts. His family was called Martha, George, and Junior. Only I called them Idiot, Liar, and Little Vomit. You see they were killing him, and I could see it. One day I noticed that something was wrong with the other people around here. Nobody's energy was right and everybody was hesitating all the time. I get these feelings, you know. I call it 'the big wind,' and I got one about this guy's family. Well finally something had to be done. What I did was this: we took the photo from him and sent him up to the orange room and really gave him the maximum session. Sixteen hours of straight friendship. We gave him the Absolute Love Beating which is the highest level of friendship-violence. And while we were doing it we called each other Martha, George, and Junior. Pretty soon he saw that it wasn't us doing it, it was his family. You know, the old misery-world clan. And when he saw that, he got the transmission all at once. Do you see what I'm getting at?"

"Listen, Buddy," Mandy said. "I got into this thing because you seemed to have some unique ideas about the universe and some interesting diet-tips and stuff. But I don't give a shit about this guy and his photo. I didn't hear anything about a dog in that photo! Let me tell you something about my dog: I took him to Dolores Park and he made friends with a goose! Have you ever seen a dog do anything like that? Bubbles should be the one giving the transmissions! That goose followed him for two blocks!"

"Let me tell you another story..." Miller started in.

And this was the moment I have been talking about. The *fulcrum* moment. Mandy could have gone one way or the other with this nutjob. And I am not pretending to be a hero—it could have just as easily been me in her shoes and her tipping the fulcrum. But it wasn't. Somehow I acted. For once. And what

I did was not much. I got up and walked over to where she was sitting. People were still stunned by the overall interruption to Miller's usual magic spell so nobody stopped me. The feeling in the air crashed even more when I broke the spatial order. Now Miller was talking again. His voice droned on behind me. He may very well have been telling me not to get up, or summoning other men to take me to the Orange Room. I was indifferent and I could no longer hear him. I walked through the smoke as if through a tunnel. It was silent. She looked up at me from her seat. Mandy and I were alone in the communion of infinite skepticism. I spoke quietly and quickly, knowing that I could be interrupted at any second.

"Look, Mandy. This transmission—I mean it's fine and everything. I just don't really like smoke, or houses, or bathrobes... I mean, I don't really know what's going on here. But I have to get out. I can't stand it. I'll tell you what: why don't we just go do something normal for a few hours, you know, like get lunch or take the dog out or something, and if you want you can come back, but I'm done with it. Do you want to go to Lazlo's or something and just think about this? You could come back tomorrow if you want."

Miller was still talking and gesticulating in the background.

"Yeah—I suppose. But I'm not recommitting to the misery-life just yet," she said.

"Fine. I'm just talking about having a few gin and tonics and walking the dog, Bubbles."

"Okay."

I could see relief on her face. She got out of her chair and we made our way through the seats toward the front door. People around us were horrified as they watched us destroy the world.

"Wait!" shouted Heliotrope. Her face was red and she looked wild-eyed. Her neck and dress were smudged with ashes.

Mandy, now resolved, turned on her with sudden menace. "Don't fuck with me, bitch!"

"No—we want to come with you!"

Filament got up from his chair and joined Heliotrope. "We're embroiled," he explained. Without another word the four of us walked toward the front door. I turned and took a last look at the red eyed group and at Miller standing in front of the crowd in his pitch-stained bathrobe. His expression was unreadable behind the sunglasses. He looked as though he had spent his entire life in the cloud of black smoke that was killing the room, a red monk of the ruins.

"You'll never be saints," he pronounced as we walked out the door and shut it behind us.

Once outside we all moved quickly. "We better get out of here before his thugs get done dealing with that coughing guy," Filament said. We got into Heliotrope's car and drove back down the hill.

Our new friends still had apartments in Berkeley, but they offered to drive Mandy and I over to her house in the city. We chatted a little bit about this and that along the way. The sun was out and the wind blasted through the little sedan as we cruised over the Bay Bridge. Mandy and I sat in the back seat. She put her head on my shoulder and I laid my arm behind it. As we traveled across the bridge I thought about what Miller had said: "You'll never be saints." He was right, of course.

We got to Mandy's place. Jennifer and Clayton (their real names) dropped us off, saying they were grateful to us for "deprogramming them," but I told them we couldn't take any credit. It wasn't independence of thought that allowed them to get out of that joint, but simply the fact that they were desperate to fuck each other—you could see it.

Mandy and I went in and greeted the dog. Bubbles leaped up into Mandy's arms. Mandy turned the television on. A true crime documentary droned along with the usual resolve. We took a shower. We had sex in there. The dog ran around and pushed its head past the curtain into the shower at one point. Then we got out. I was unhappy to have to put clothes on that still smelled like smoke. She made coffee. We drank it and then took the dog up to Dolores Park.

Later at Lazlo's, Mandy drank gin and I drank Scotch. The African music was humming away from the juke box. Neither of us said much for about five minutes. It was pleasant. Finally, Mandy spoke up.

"What do you think of those big, soft pretzels?"

"I don't eat that shit."

"Why not?"

"Because it's not even food. Those things are just like—I don't know, like weird bread-balls or something."

"YOU'RE a weird bread-ball."

"That doesn't even make sense."

She reached down and yanked one of my shoelaces untied and left it hanging there.